To: James
From: schuyler

W9-BYA-557

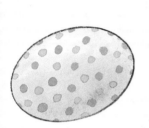

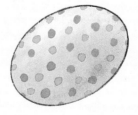

Based on the television series *The Wubbulous World of Dr. Seuss*™.
Produced by Jim Henson Productions in association with Nickelodeon.

Copyright © 1996 Jim Henson Productions, Inc.
THE CAT IN THE HAT, THE GRINCH, HORTON THE ELEPHANT, THIDWICK THE BIG-HEARTED MOOSE,
and NORVAL THE FISH character names and designs © & ™ Dr. Seuss Enterprises, L.P.
THE WUBBULOUS WORLD OF DR. SEUSS is a trademark of Dr. Seuss Enterprises, L.P.,
under exclusive license to Jim Henson Productions, Inc.
All rights reserved under International and Pan-American Copyright Conventions.
Published in the United States by Random House, Inc., New York, and simultaneously
in Canada by Random House of Canada Limited, Toronto.

http://www.randomhouse.com/

Library of Congress Cataloging-in-Publication Data
Rabe, Tish.   The song of the Zubble-wump /
by Tish Rabe ; adapted from a script by David Steven Cohen ; illustrated by Tom Brannon.
p.   cm. — (The wubbulous world of Dr. Seuss)
SUMMARY: Seven-year-old Megan and Horton the Elephant set off to rescue the Zubble-wump egg
when it is taken by the Grinch.
ISBN 0-679-88419-X (trade) — ISBN 0-679-98419-4 (lib. bdg.)
[1. Eggs—Fiction.   2. Elephants—Fiction.   3. Stories in rhyme.]
I. Cohen, David Steven, 1943-   .   II. Brannon, Tom, ill.   III. Title.   IV. Series.
PZ8.3.R1145So   1996   [E]—dc20   96-35011

Printed in the United States of America   10 9 8 7 6 5 4 3 2 1

The Wubbulous world of Dr. Seuss™

The Song of the Zubble-wump

by Tish Rabe

adapted from a script by David Steven Cohen

illustrated by Tom Brannon

RANDOM HOUSE/
JIM HENSON PRODUCTIONS

Welcome, my friends, to a wubbulous place,
a truly stupendous, spectacular space.
Where you never have worries or pies in your face,
and mistakes that you make you can change or erase.

It was here something happened—of this there's no doubt—
to an egg that the world simply can't live without.

A one-of-a-kind egg, I'm sure you can tell,
a too-hard-to-find egg—for inside its shell
lies a secret you can't buy and no one can sell,
as Megan Mullally and Grandpa know well.

"Grandpa," sighed Megan, "this wait is too great!
I've been waiting my whole life—and I'm almost eight."

"Hang on," Grandpa said, "for tomorrow's the date.
It will hatch right on time, not a minute too late.
But till then just Mullallys
may touch it, it's true.
And Mullally means me,
and Mullally means you—
and nobody else,
no matter who."

"I'll guard it," said Megan, "I won't sleep all night.
And if someone comes near it, they're in for a fight."

"You are brave," Grandpa said, "but a girl needs her rest.
And so, for this job, I've invited a guest."

"I'm Horton the Elephant—
here at your service!
I've watched lots of eggs.
There's no need to be nervous.
I love to help out,
and it's great fun to visit.
I'll tend to your egg,
but please tell me—
what is it?"

"This egg," Grandpa said, "from the Zubbulous Valley,
belonged years ago to my Grandpa Mullally
and his Great-Great-Grandpa's
Great-Great-Great-Great-Grandpa's
Great-Great-Great-Great-Grandpa's Great-Grandmother Sally.
It hatches just once every eighty-two years,
and it's well worth the wait for your eyes and your ears!
For inside this shell's a miraculous thing
that will whistle and warble and splendidly sing
a song that is fit for the ears of a king."

"What is it?" asked Horton. "What is this fine thing?"

"This egg is not fish, fowl, nor double-hump camel;
not lizard, nor leopard, nor muskox, nor mammal.
Nor buffalo herd, nor huffalo bird.
In fact, for this egg there is only one word,
and that's…
ZUBBLE-WUMP."

"A Zubble-wump! Wow!"
Horton gasped. "Can it be?
That they really exist—
and not just on TV?
I will stay here to guard it and watch through the night
to make sure that this most precious egg is all right.
No villain will shiver or quiver or shake it.
This egg's like my promise and nothing will break it!"

So all through the night,
Horton watched it steadfastly...

But something was coming—so ghoulish, so ghastly,
so fearsomely, fiercely, ferociously foul,
with its screechily, scratchily, scabby crab scowl.
Something creaky and sneaky and slitherly slivious
crept to where Horton (completely oblivious)
sat, while two hands that were not very clean
switched the Zubble-wump egg—

for an egg that was GREEN!

When Megan woke up, she cried out in dismay,
"Someone's stolen our egg! It's been taken away!"

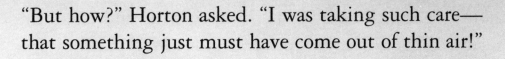

"But how?" Horton asked. "I was taking such care—
that something just must have come out of thin air!"

But it wasn't a Grinkle, a Groog, or a Grax,
or a Wabsidon Wog, with its ears full of wax.
Whoever had stolen the egg had left tracks.
Great green grubby tracks, as a matter of facts!

"I've seen these before," Grandpa gasped, "in my youth!
They were left there by something so cruel and uncouth
that it scared all the hair off dear Aunt Mary Ruth.
The Grinch left those tracks! I'm afraid it's the truth!"

"The Grinch stole our egg?" Megan cried. "Well, he'll see
he can't sneak in and steal from Mullallys like me.
That grime-slimy Grinch! I don't care if he's mean!
I'll get our egg back from that rotten green bean."

"Now that," Grandpa said,
"I just can't let you do.
Our egg may be lost,
but I can't lose *you,* too!
That Grinch is all broken, that Grinch is all bent.
His heart's full of hurt and his soul is cement."

"This theft," Horton said, "was my job to prevent.
I will go get your egg back, one hundred percent."

So Horton set out for the dreaded Grinch Grotto.
"I mean what I say" was this elephant's motto.
But just then he heard a strange flippy-flap sound.
"Who is it?" asked Horton, not turning around.
"Who goes there? Who are you? Please make yourself known.
On second thought, stay there and leave me alone."

"It's me!" Megan cried. "I left Grandpa a note!"
"You're here!" Horton croaked past the lump in his throat.
"Come on!" Megan urged. "As a team we're a cinch.
We can get my egg back from that grabby old Grinch."

So they set out together down Mustydust Road,
past a moose who was carrying quite a strange load.
Through Jingaboo Jungle, where Jurgles lay lurking,
down Gobbed-with-Goo River, where Smurgers were smirking,
past a wood filled with holly, where no one was working.
And on through the Valley of Hard-to-Breathe Air,
the girl and the elephant tiptoed with care,
so they wouldn't wake up the Slugubrious Slime,
who likes to sleep deep every day until nine.

Then Megan and Horton,
hearts heavy with dread,
trying hard not to guess
where the rocky path led,
walked on till they saw
on a hill
up ahead
a sight that would fright
anyone who's not dead.
At the far nearest side
of the Whezzlebeeze Wood,
where the Whezzlebeeze live
and are up to no good,
there the Grinch Grotto stood,
where no other thing could.
It was eerie and smeary,
its walls caked with muck.
It was squoozing and oozing
with grinchy green guck.

"Here I go!" Horton cried.
"Wish me speed, wish me luck."
But the path was too thin
and poor Horton...

...got stuck!

"Perhaps," Horton sighed, "I should go on a diet."
"Too late!" Megan cried. "This is no time to try it!"

The one thing to do—
it was true and she knew it—
was take her egg back.
It was *her* job to do it.

She crept slowly up
to the window and peeked.
Her shoulders were shaking,
her new sneakers squeaked.

Inside, the Grinch hunched in a bunch near his prize,
with a grin on his lips, a green gleam in his eyes.

Then Megan burst out, "Oh, you moldy cold slime.
You gimme my egg, 'cause it's mine, mine, mine, mine!
And soon it will hatch, just exactly on time."

"Your greed," the Grinch snarled,
"is quite charming, indeed!
It grows in your heart
like a wicked old weed."

"You Grinch!" Megan cried.
"You're a smear and a smudge!"
"My dear," the Grinch sneered,
"you're a fine one to judge.
You're as seedy and needy and greedy as me."
"I'm not," Megan yelled. "NO, THAT SIMPLY CAN'T BE!"

"And this egg," screeched the Grinch with an eek-squeaky whine,
"is a Grumble-up egg—and it's mine, mine, all mine!"
"No, it's not!" Megan shouted. "It belongs all to me!
It's a Zubble-wump egg, as the whole world can see.
And I'm taking it back, just as back as can be."

So she grabbed up the egg,
but the Grinch grabbed it, too.
"It is mine!" they both cried.
"Me means *me* and not you!"

"It is mine!"

"No, it's mine!"

"No,
it's mine, mine,
mine, mine."

"It is mine, mine, mine,
mine, mine, mine,
mine, mine,
mine,
mine!!!"

They tugged and they tussled,
they grappled and grasped.
Till it slipped from their grip.
"My egg!" Megan gasped.

It flipped fifty somersaults,
up and around,
till it smashed into smithereens—
crash!—
on the ground.

"Oh, no!" Megan cried. "Oh, what have we done?
That Zubble-wump egg was the very last one!
Now I never will hear the sweet Zubble-wump's song!"

"Blame yourself," cried the Grinch.
"It's your fault; you were wrong.
You grabbed for the egg, and you caused it to fall.
Now that it's broken, it's no use at all."

"You *both* are to blame," said a voice, "it's quite clear.
I'm the Cat in the Hat, and you've nothing to fear.
I know Mister Grinch, and I knew what he'd do.
He'd sneak in and try the old Egg Switcheroo.
So I switcherooed first, and when he came creeping,
the Zubble-wump egg was with *me* for safekeeping!
And as for you, Megan, you seem to forget
that egg is a miracle, not just a pet."

Megan reached for the egg, but the Cat said, "One minute!
This egg's holding something important within it.
A beauty so rare it cannot be compared.
A gift such as this one is meant to be shared."

Then they stopped,
for they heard
a strange scritching and scratching.
A scribble, a scrabble, a hitching—
a hatching!

The egg cracked with a creak—
and out poked a small beak.
"It's here," Megan whispered.
She scarcely could speak.

Then she smiled and gazed into the Zubble-wump's eyes,
and there she discovered a joyous surprise,
as the Zubble-wump puffed up its Zubbulous chest
and sang out the song Zubble-wumps sing the best.
A song clear as air, sweet as fresh mountain streams,
a song that sprang straight from her very own dreams!

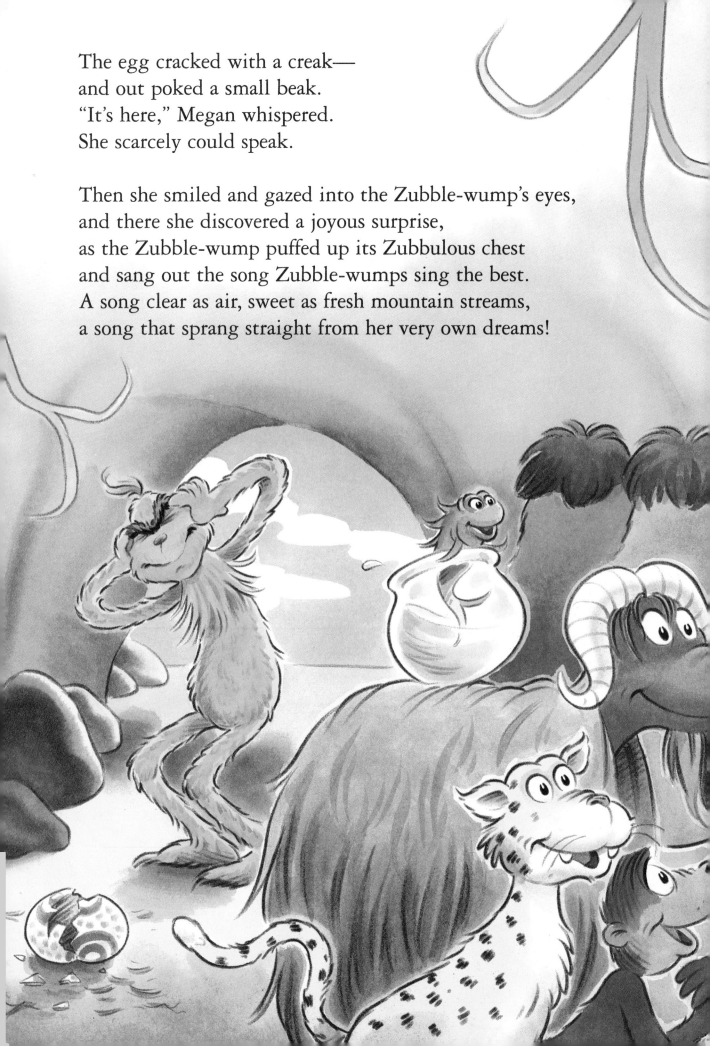

And everyone, everywhere, heard the song soar.
And it wasn't like songs they'd been hearing before.
It filled up the world where there once had been space,
bringing peace to sore hearts and a smile to each face.

Which is why the Grinch hated it right from the start.
That song was a dagger aimed straight at his heart.
"Stop!" the Grinch cried. "Do not sing one more note.
Someone go stuff a sock in that Zubble-wump's throat."

Then over the hill at a madcapping pace
came a dearly familiar and worried old face.
"You were gone!" Grandpa cried.
"But I knew where you'd be!"
"I'm fine," Megan piped.
"Just as fine as can be.
But the Zubble-wump is
even finer, you see.
By the good name Mullally,
I'm setting it…

"I've learned something new
that I now know is true:

A Zubble-wump's lovely with just two ears hearing,
but more ears give more of a reason for cheering.
With sixty or eighty, two thousand and ten,
the pleasure is doubled again and again.
And again and again and again and again
and twice double that and again some—amen."

Oh, and as for the Grinch—well, last time we heard news,
he was up to his ears in thick Ooblecky Ooze,
trying hard not to hear the sweet Zubble-wump's song.
But you all know the Grinch.
He'll be back
before long.